Wee Sing and Play ®

Musical games and rhymes for children

by
Pamela Conn Beall
and
Susan Hagen Nipp

Illustrated
by
Nancy Spence Klein

PRICE STERN SLOAN
Los Angeles

To our friends of tradition . . .

(and to OUR old favorites,
Ron and Charlie)

Copyright©1981 by Pamela Conn Beall and Susan Hagen Nipp
Published by Price Stern Sloan, Inc.
11150 Olympic Boulevard, Suite 650
Los Angeles, California 90064

ISBN:0-8431-0391-4

PSS! ® and Wee Sing ® are registered trademarks of Price Stern Sloan, Inc.

30 29 28 27

PREFACE

"Me first! Me first!" "There's nothing to do!" "What can we play at the party?" "This is boring."

Have you ever encountered any of these situations and been at a loss for a solution? What about turning to your own childhood days for assistance? Our heritage is rich with children's games and rhymes that have survived the years and are still loved in our contemporary world. We can appreciate them even more by realizing that, beyond enjoyment, a child is developing skills in the areas of coordination, rhythm, singing, creative imagination, following directions and fair play.

Areas covered in *Wee Sing and Play* include choosing rhymes to determine fairly who's first, circle and singing games for enjoyment in group situations, jump rope and ball bouncing rhymes which produce a great sense of satisfaction when mastered, and clapping games to challenge any child. The criteria for selection included expression of music or rhythm, American heritage and familiarity.

An exciting process occurs when traditions are kept alive. We hope through *Wee Sing and Play* you will share and enjoy this wonderful heritage with your children and that they, in turn, will continue the process.

Pam Beall
Susan Nipp

TABLE OF CONTENTS

"I can jump in . . . but how do I get out?"
JUMP ROPE RHYMES   35

"Bounce and turn at the same time? . . . You're kidding!"
BALL BOUNCING RHYMES   43

"Clap faster AND in rhythm? . . . Who me?"
CLAPPING RHYMES   51

Me first! Me first!.....
There must be a better way.

Choosing rhymes

Choosing rhymes determine who is "it." One of the group chants the rhyme while pointing to the children one by one, including himself. By one method, the child pointed to on the last word is "it." By another, he is out and the rhyme is repeated until one child is left to be "it." Mother Goose rhymes can also be used as choosing rhymes.

EENY, MEENY, MINY, MO

Eeny, meeny, miny, mo,
　　Catch a tiger by the toe.
If he hollers, make him pay
　　Fifty dollars every day.
My mother told me to
　　Choose the very best one.

Variation:

Eeny, meeny, miny, mo,
　　Catch a rabbit by the toe.
If he hollers, let him go,
　　Eeny, meeny, miny, mo.

ICKY BICKY

Icky, bicky soda cracker,
　　Icky, bicky boo,
Icky, bicky soda cracker,
　　Out goes you!

HOT POTATO

One potato, two potato,
 Three potato, four,
Five potato, six potato,
 Seven potato, MORE.

Formation: Children stand in circle or line with fists held out in front of them. One child is "it."

Action: "It" pounds each fist in turn, including his own, in rhythm. The fist pounded on "MORE" is placed behind that child's back. This continues until one fist remains. That child is the winner.

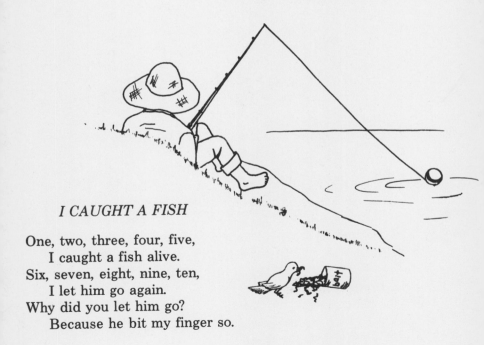

I CAUGHT A FISH

One, two, three, four, five,
 I caught a fish alive.
Six, seven, eight, nine, ten,
 I let him go again.
Why did you let him go?
 Because he bit my finger so.

APPLES, PEACHES

Apples, peaches, pears, and plums,
    Tell me when your birthday comes.

"March"   M-A-R-C-H

Variation: "March" January, February, March

The child pointed to on "comes" names
the month of his birthday and the
rhyme continues as above.

FIREMAN, FIREMAN

Fireman, fireman, number eight,
    Hit his head against the gate.
The gate flew in, the gate flew out,
    That's how he put the fire out.
O-U-T spells OUT
    And out you go.

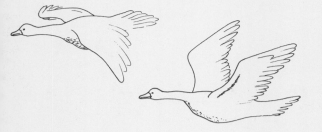

ONE TWO

One, two
    Sky blue
All out (in)
    But you!

ENTRY, KENTRY

Entry, Kentry, cutry, corn,
    Apple seed and apple thorn
Wire, brier, limber lock
    Three geese in a flock.
One flew east, one flew west,
    One flew over the cuckoo's nest.
O-U-T spells out goes she (he).

A, B, C, D

A, b, c, d, e, f, g,
    h, i, j, k, l, m, n, o, p,
        q, r, s, t,
            U are out!

MARY AT THE KITCHEN DOOR

One, two, three, four,
    Mary at the kitchen door.
Five, six, seven, eight,
    Mary at the garden gate.
O-U-T spells out!

BUBBLE GUM

Bubble gum, bubble gum in a dish,
   How many pieces do you wish?

"Five"   1, 2, 3, 4, 5 and out you go.

The child pointed to on "wish" answers with a number
and the rhyme continues by counting to that number.

Suggestions: Fists in front can be pounded.

ENGINE NUMBER 9

Engine, engine, Number Nine,
   Going down Chicago Line.
If the train goes off the track,
   Do you want your money back?

"No"   N-O spells no, and out you go!

or

"Yes"   Y-E-S spells yes and out you go!

The child pointed to on "back" answers "yes"
or "no" and the rhyme continues by spelling
that word as above.

It's party time......Now what?

Circle and singing games

THE FARMER IN THE DELL

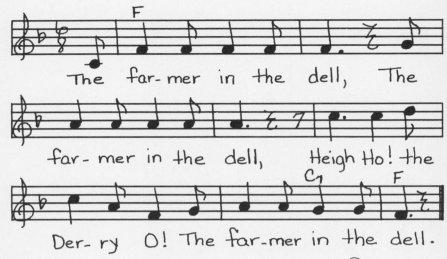

The far-mer in the dell, The far-mer in the dell, Heigh Ho! the Der-ry O! The far-mer in the dell.

2. The farmer takes the wife
3. The wife takes the child
4. The child takes the nurse
5. The nurse takes the dog
6. The dog takes the cat
7. The cat takes the rat
8. The rat takes the cheese
9. The cheese stands alone

Formation: Circle, hands joined.
One child, the "farmer," in center.

Action: Children circle around the farmer. Verse 2, the farmer chooses a wife to join him in the center of circle. The game is continued until the last verse when all but the cheese return to the circle. The cheese becomes the farmer for the new game.

Suggestion: Those inside circle may march or circle around within the larger circle.

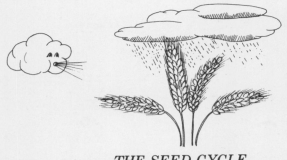

THE SEED CYCLE
(Tune: The Farmer in the Dell)

1. The farmer sows his seeds . . . Heigh Ho!
   the Derry O! The farmer sows his seeds.
   (Seeds curl up on the ground)
2. The wind begins to blow . . .
   (Wind players run about waving arms)
3. The rain begins to fall . . .
   (Rain players run about, fingers hanging
   down to indicate raindrops)
4. The sun begins to shine . . .
   (Sun players walk slowly, arms in circle
   above head)
5. The seeds begin to grow . . .
   (Seed players slowly rise, becoming grain)
6. The farmer cuts his grain . . .
   (Action as with scythe; grain falls to ground)
7. The farmer binds his sheaves . . .
   (Farmer touches three at a time, who
   stand back to back)
8. And now the harvest's in . . .
   (All skip around sheaves, hands joined)

Formation: Before song is begun, divide group into seeds, wind, rain, suns, and one farmer. Form large circle. Inside circle are seeds and farmer.

Action: Each group pantomimes words of song and returns to place except seeds who always remain in center.

Suggestion: Simplify by having all children pantomime all parts.

THE NOBLE DUKE OF YORK
or A-HUNTING WE WILL GO

Oh, the no-ble Duke of York, He had ten thous-and men; He marched them up to the top of the hill and marched them down a-gain.

2. And when you're up, you're up,
   And when you're down, you're down,
   And when you're only half way up,
   You're neither up nor down.

3. Oh, a-hunting we will go,
   A-hunting we will go;
   We'll catch a little fox and put
   him in a box
   And then we'll let him go.

GAME 1

Use verses 1 and 2.

Formation: Sitting in chairs or squatting.

Action: Verse 1
   "10,000 men" – raise arms full length
                            fingers outstretched
   "up" –   stand
   "down" –   sit

Verse 2   Repeat actions for "up" and "down."
On "halfway" – assume crouching position

A-HUNTING WE WILL GO
GAME 2

Use verses 1 and 3.

Formation: Circle, hands joined. One child
as the "fox" stands outside circle.

Action: Verse 1
Children circle to left as fox skips to right.

Verse 3
The two children nearest the fox lift arms and force him into circle
by bringing arch down on other side of him. Children slowly close
circle to trap fox. On "let him go," children raise arms and let fox
escape. He chooses another fox and the game begins again.

GAME 3

Use verse 3.

Formation: Form a line of pairs with a head couple.

Action: Head couple leads partners as they march across room,
separating at the end, one line going right and the other left. Lines
march back to the other end where partners meet. The head
couple forms an arch through which the other couples march. This
creates a new head couple and the game continues until all
children have been head couple.

PUNCHINELLO

What can you do, Pun-chi-nel-lo fun-ny fel-low?

What can you do, Pun-chi-nel-lo fun-ny you?

2. We can do it, too . . .
3. You choose one of us . . .

Formation: Circle, one child in center as Punchinello

Action: Verse 1
Punchinello makes a motion as children sing.

Verse 2

Children in circle copy motion of Punchinello.

Verse 3

Punchinello chooses another to be in center and takes that person's place in the circle.

THE HOKEY-POKEY

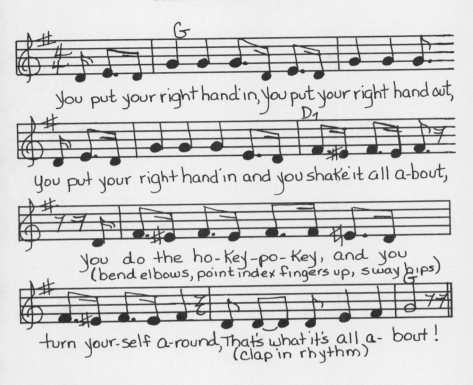

You put your right hand in, You put your right hand out,
You put your right hand in and you shake it all a-bout,
You do the ho-key-po-key, and you
(bend elbows, point index fingers up, sway hips)
turn your-self a-round, That's what it's all a-bout!
(clap in rhythm)

2. You put your left hand in . . .
3. Right foot in
4. Left foot in
5. Right shoulder in
6. Left shoulder in
7. Right hip in
8. Left hip in
9. Head in
10. Whole self in

Formation: Circle

Action: Follow action of the words.

THE MUFFIN MAN

Oh, do you know the muf-fin man, the muf-fin man, the muf-fin man, Oh do you know the muf-fin man, Who lives on Dru-ry Lane?

2. Oh, yes, I know the muffin man.
3. Now four of us know the muffin man.
4. Now we all know the muffin man,

GAME 1

Formation: Circle hands joined, one child in center.

Action: Verse 1
Children circle around child. At end of verse child chooses a partner.

Verse 2
Children circle around. At end of verse, the two in center choose two more.

Verse 3
Circle. At the end of verse, choose four more. Repeat verse 3 changing the number each time until all are in the center.

Verse 4
All children circle round.

THE MUFFIN MAN
GAME 2

Formation: Circle. One child is blindfolded in center.

Action: Verse 1
Group sings as they circle around blindfolded child.

Verse 2
Stop circling. Chosen one of group sings alone.

The blindfolded child guesses who sang alone. Soloist then becomes blindfolded child.

SALLY GO 'ROUND THE SUN

Formation: Circle, holding hands.

Action: Circle around. On "BOOM," jump up and reverse direction to immediately start singing song again.

DROP THE HANDKERCHIEF

(Tune: Yankee Doodle)

I wrote a let-ter to my love and on the way I dropped it, A lit-tle dog-gie picked it up and put it in his pock-et, And he won't bite you, And he but he will bite you! (spoken)

Formation: Circle. One child is "it" and stands outside the circle holding a handkerchief.

Action: As children sing the first three lines, "it" walks around the circle. "It" sings or chants the last line until he decides to drop the handkerchief behind a child and say "but he will bite you." He then races around the circle back to the empty space. The new child picks up the handkerchief and runs in the opposite direction, also racing to the space. After the race, the new child then becomes "it."

'ROUND THE VILLAGE

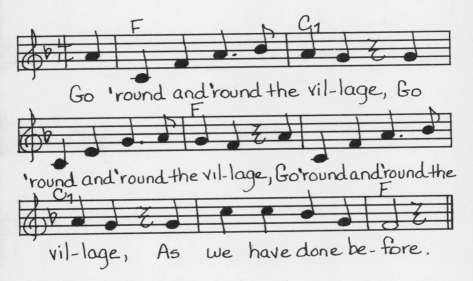

Go 'round and 'round the vil-lage, Go 'round and 'round the vil-lage, Go 'round and 'round the vil-lage, As we have done be-fore.

2. Go in and out the window . . .
3. Now come and face your partner
4. Now follow me to London

Formation: Circle, hands joined. "It" stands outside the circle.

Action: V.1 – "It" skips or runs around circle.
V.2 – Children in circle raise arms to form arches while "it" weaves in and out.
V.3 – "It" chooses a partner and stands facing him.
V.4 – "It" leads partner in and out of circle.
V.1 – "It" returns to circle and partner becomes "it."

Suggestion: For shorter game, use only verses
2 and 3. Partner immediately becomes "it."

LONDON BRIDGE

Lon-don bridge is fal-ling down, fal-ling down,

fal-ling down, Lon-don bridge is fal-ling down,

My fair la-dy.

Chorus: (sung after each verse)
    Take the key and lock her up . . .
2. Build it up with iron bars
3. Iron bars will bend and break
4. Build it up with silver and gold

LONDON BRIDGE

GAME 1

Formation: Two children join hands and form an arch. They secretly decide who is silver and who is gold. The other children form a single line to pass under the bridge.

Action:

V.1 — Children in line pass under bridge. On "My fair lady," the bridge falls and captures a prisoner.

Chorus — The bridge gently sways the prisoner back and forth. At the end of the chorus, the prisoner is secretly asked, "Do you want to pay with silver or gold?" The prisoner then stands behind the child representing his choice. The game continues with verses and chorus until all children have been captured. A tug-of-war between "gold" and "silver" ends the game.

Suggestion: You may choose other forms of payment such as cake or ice cream, marbles or jacks, etc.

GAME 2

Formation: Same as Game 1.

Action: Same as Game 1 through the choice of "silver or gold." At this point, the prisoner takes the place in the bridge of the child representing his choice. The child who was part of the bridge joins the line and the game continues.

BLUE BIRD

Blue-bird, blue-bird, through my win-dow,

Blue-bird, blue-bird, through my win-dow,

Blue-bird, blue-bird, through my win-dow,

Oh, John-ny, I am tired.

Formation: Circle, hands joined and raised to form arches. One child, the "bluebird," stands outside circle.

Action: The bluebird weaves in and out of circle. On "Oh, Johnny, I am tired," he taps another child on the shoulder. The child tapped becomes the new bird as the first child takes his place in the circle.

Suggestion: Let the new child choose what kind of bird he wants to be.

THE MERRY-GO-ROUND

(Tune: Mulberry Bush)

The mer-ry-go-round goes round and round, The chil-dren laughed and laughed and laughed, So man-y were go-ing round and round that the mer-ry-go-round col-lapsed.

Formation: Circle, hands joined.

Action: Circle around while singing. On the word "collapsed," all fall down.

DID YOU EVER SEE A LASSIE?

GAME 1

Formation: Circle, holding hands. One child in center.

Action: Children circle around lassie (laddie). On the words "this way and that," the lassie performs an action of her choosing. The other children stop circling and imitate the action until the end of the song. The lassie chooses a new child and the game continues.

GAME 2

In place of the word "lassie," the child chooses what he wants to be, such as a farmer (pretend to feed chickens), airplane (fly), tree (sway gently), elephant (swing trunk).

JIMMY CRACK CORN

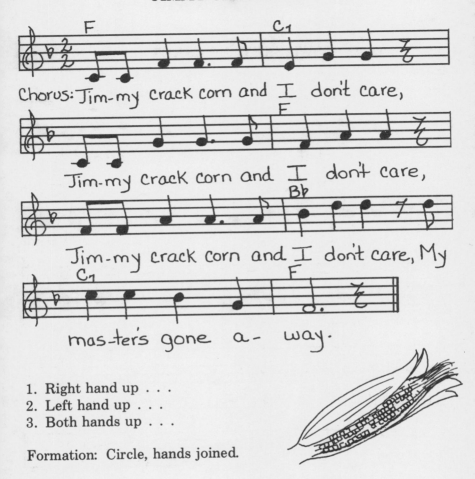

Chorus: Jim-my crack corn and I don't care,
Jim-my crack corn and I don't care,
Jim-my crack corn and I don't care, My
mas-ter's gone a- way.

1. Right hand up . . .
2. Left hand up . . .
3. Both hands up . . .

Formation: Circle, hands joined.

Action:
Chorus (do after each verse) – circle to left
V.1 – with right hand raised, move to center
       of circle, touch hands and move back
       quickly on "My master's gone away."
V.2 – same as v.1, using left hand
V.3 – same as v.1, using both hands

A-TISKET, A-TASKET

A - tis-ket, a-tas-ket, a green and yel-low
bas-ket, I wrote a let-ter to my love and
on the way I dropped it. I dropped it, I
dropped it, and on the way I dropped it, A
lit-tle boy picked it up and put it in his pock-et.
(girl)   (her)

Formation: Circle. One child is chosen to be "it" and stands outside the circle holding a handkerchief.

Action: As children sing, "it" skips around the outside of the circle. Sometime during the words "I dropped it," "it" drops the handkerchief behind any child he chooses. He then races around the circle back to the empty space. The new child picks up the handkerchief and runs in the opposite direction, also racing to the space. After the race, the new child then becomes "it."

SKIP TO MY LOU

Lost my part-ner, what'll I do? Lost my part-ner, what'll I do? Lost my part-ner, what'll I do? Skip to my Lou, my dar-ling.

Chorus (to be sung after each verse):
    Lou, Lou, skip to my Lou . . .
    Skip to my Lou, my darling.
2. I'll get another, a better one too;
3. Can't get a redbird, a bluebird'll do;
4. Cat's in the buttermilk, skip to my Lou;
5. Flies in the sugar bowl, shoo, fly, shoo.

Formation: Circle, one child is "it" inside circle.

Action:
V.1 – Children sing and clap as "it" skips inside circle. On "Skip to my Lou, my darling," "it" chooses a partner.
Chorus – "It" and partner skip inside circle holding hands. On "Skip to my Lou, my darling," "it" returns to circle and partner becomes new "it."
    Continue game with verse 2.

OATS, PEAS, BEANS

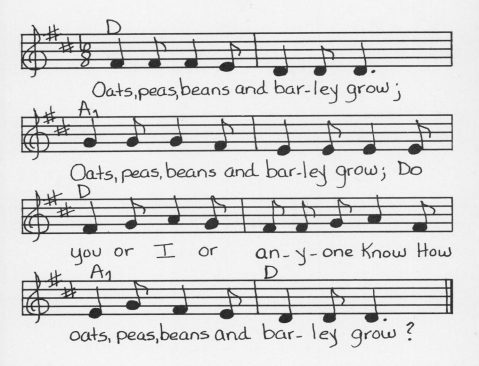

Oats, peas, beans and bar-ley grow;

Oats, peas, beans and bar-ley grow; Do

you or I or an-y-one know how

oats, peas, beans and bar-ley grow?

2. First the farmer sows his seed,
Then he stands and takes his ease:
    (fold arms)
Stamps his foot and claps his hand,
And turns around to view the land.
    (shade eyes)
3. Waiting for a partner,
Waiting for a partner,
Open the ring and take one in,
And then we'll gaily dance and sing.
4. Tra la la la la la la,

Formation: Circle, with hands joined.
Farmer stands in center.

Action: Verse 1
Children circle to left. Farmer walks
inside circle to right.

Verse 2

Farmer and children act out words.

Verse 3

Children in circle stand and clap hands
as the farmer chooses a partner.

Verse 4

Farmer and partner skip to right inside
circle. Children join hands and circle
to left. To play again, the partner becomes the new farmer.

33

OLD BRASS WAGON

Cir-cle to the left, the old brass wa-gon;

Cir-cle to the left, the old brass wa-gon;

Cir-cle to the left, the old brass wa-gon;

You're the one my dar-ling.

2. Circle to the right . . .
3. Everybody in
4. Everybody out

Formation: Circle, hands joined.
Action:
V. 1 & 2 – follow directions of song
V.3 – walk to center of circle, moving
hands forward and up
V.4 – walk backwards, extending hands
to the rear
At conclusion of song, everyone bows.

Suggestion: Make up own directions such as
tiptoe, skip, hop.

I can jump in....
but how do I get out?

Jump rope rhymes

Most jump rope rhymes are chanted as two children turn a rope and a third jumps. However, many rhymes are appropriate for the individual jumper with his own rope. Some rhymes specify actions which the jumper must perform. Other rhymes ask a question and the number or word on which the jumper misses determines the answer. Nursery rhymes may be used as a rhythmic chant while jumping.

ALL IN TOGETHER, GIRLS

All in together, girls
    First by the weather, girls
When you call your birthday
    You must jump out.
January, February, March . . .
    (continue naming months)

CINDERELLA

Cinderella dressed in yellow,
    Went downstairs to kiss her fellow.
How many kisses did she get?
    One, two, three . . .
        (continue counting)

Cinderella dressed in lace,
    Went upstairs to powder her face.
How many pounds did it take?
    One, two, three . . .

Cinderella dressed in red,
    Went downstairs to bake some bread.
How many loaves did she bake?
    One, two, three . . .

TWO LITTLE SAUSAGES

Two little sausages
   Frying in a pan,
One went pop
   And the other went bam!
      (Two children jumping. One
      jumps out on "pop," the other
      on "bam." Two more jump in
      to continue chant.)

MABEL, MABEL

Mabel, Mabel, set the table,
   Just as fast as you are able.
Don't forget the salt, sugar, vinegar . . .
     (continue naming things until
     ready for peppers)
And don't forget the RED HOT PEPPERS!
     (jump as fast as possible)

DUTCH GIRL

I'm a little Dutch Girl
   Dressed in blue;
And these are the things
   I like to do;
Salute to the Captain,
   Bow to the Queen,
And turn my back
   To the submarine.

LITTLE SPANISH DANCER

Not last night but the night before,
    Twenty-four robbers came knockin' at my door,
As I ran out, they ran in,
        (jumper runs out, then in again)
    And this is what they told me:
Little Spanish dancer, do the splits,
    Little Spanish dancer do high kicks,
Little Spanish dancer, touch the ground,
    Little Spanish dancer, get out of town.
        (jumper runs out)

I LOVE COFFEE

I love coffee,
    I love tea,
I want *Mary*
    To come in with me.

DOWN IN THE VALLEY

Down in the valley
    Where the green grass grows,
There sat *Susie*
    As pretty as a rose;
She sang, she sang,
    She sang so sweet,
Along came *Johnny*
    And kissed her on the cheek.
How many kisses did she get?
    One, two, three . . .
        (continue counting)

TEDDY BEAR

Teddy Bear, Teddy Bear,
  Turn around,
Teddy Bear, Teddy Bear,
  Touch the ground,
Teddy Bear, Teddy Bear,
  Show your shoe,
Teddy Bear, Teddy Bear,
  That will do!

Teddy Bear, Teddy Bear,
  Go upstairs,
Teddy Bear, Teddy Bear,
  Say your prayers,
Teddy Bear, Teddy Bear,
  Switch off the light,
Teddy Bear, Teddy Bear,
  Say good-night.

I LIKE COFFEE

I like coffee, I like tea,
  I like the boys and the boys like me.
Yes, no, maybe so . . .

BLUEBELLS, COCKLE SHELLS

Bluebells, cockle shells,
  Eevy, ivy, over.
(Rope is swung back and forth until "over"
when it goes full circle in hot peppers.)

MISS LUCY HAD A BABY

Miss Lucy had a baby,
    (one child jumping)
  His name was Tiny Tim,
She put him in the bathtub
    To see if he could swim.
He drank up all the water,
    He ate up all the soap,
He tried to eat the bathtub,
    But it wouldn't go down his throat.
Miss Lucy called the doctor,
    (doctor runs in)
  Miss Lucy called the nurse,
    (nurse runs in)
Miss Lucy called the lady with the
  Alligator purse.
    (lady runs in)
"Mumps," said the doctor,
    (all four jump together)
  "Measles," said the nurse,
"Nothing," said the lady with the
  Alligator purse.
Miss Lucy punched the doctor,
    (doctor runs out)
  Miss Lucy knocked the nurse,
    (nurse runs out)
Miss Lucy paid the lady with the
  Alligator purse.
    (Lucy runs out and lady
    starts the rhyme again)

ICE CREAM SODA

Ice cream soda, lemonade tart,
   Tell me the name of your sweetheart.
A, B, C, D, E . . .
     (the letter on which the jumper misses
     is the first letter of the sweetheart's name)

POLLY PUT THE KETTLE ON

Polly put the kettle on
   And have a cup of tea,
In comes *Janie*
And out goes me.

KEEP THE KETTLE BOILING

Keep the kettle boiling,
   Don't you dare be late!
     (the rope keeps turning as
     jumpers run in and out
     consecutively without losing
     the rhythm.)

BREAD AND BUTTER

Bread and butter,
   Sugar and spice,
How many boys
   Think I'm nice?
One, two, three . . .
     (continue counting)

DOWN BY THE OCEAN

Down by the ocean,
　Down by the sea,
Johnny broke a bottle
　And blamed it all on me.
I told Ma,
　Ma told Pa,
Johnny got a spankin'
　So, Ha! Ha! Ha!
How many spankings did he get?
　One, two, three . . .
　　(continue counting)

MISS, MISS

Miss, miss,
　Pretty little miss,
When you miss,
　You miss like this.
　　(Stop rope)

ENGINE NUMBER NINE

Engine, engine Number Nine,
　Going down Chicago Line,
See it sparkle, see it shine,
　Engine, engine Number Nine.
If the train should jump the track,
　Will I get my money back?
Yes, no, maybe so . . .

LITTLE JUMPING JOAN

Here am I,
　Little Jumping Joan;
When nobody's with me,
　I'm all alone.

Bounce and turn at the same time?.... You're kidding!

Ball bouncing rhymes

Ball bouncing rhymes are usually used to emphasize rhythm while bouncing a ball. Most jump rope rhymes and nursery rhymes can be used for ball bouncing.

NUMBER ONE, TOUCH YOUR TONGUE

Number One, touch your tongue.
Number Two, touch your shoe.
Number Three, touch your knee.
Number Four, touch the floor.
Number Five, learn to jive.
Number Six, pick up sticks.
Number Seven, go to heaven.
Number Eight, over the gate.
Number Nine, touch your spine.
Number Ten, do it again.
(Perform actions while bouncing
ball in rhythm.)

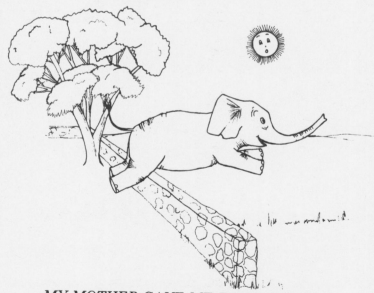

MY MOTHER GAVE ME FIFTY CENTS

My mother gave me fifty cents
To see the elephant jump the fence.
He jumped so high he reached the sky
And didn't come down till the 4th of July.

POP! GOES THE WEASEL

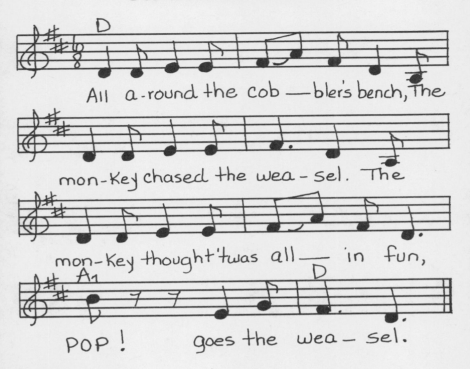

All a-round the cob —bler's bench, The
mon-key chased the wea - sel. The
mon-key thought 'twas all — in fun,
POP! goes the wea - sel.

GAME 1

Formation: Two or more players.

Action: One child bounces ball in rhythm as all sing.
On "POP!" he either passes or bounces ball to another
child who repeats the game.

GAME 2

Formation: Several players seated or standing in circle.

Action: Pass ball around circle while singing song.
On "POP!", child with ball tosses it across circle
to another player who begins the passing again.

ONE, TWO, BUCKLE MY SHOE

1, 2,
Buckle my shoe;
3, 4,
Shut the door;
5, 6,
Pick up sticks;
7, 8,
Lay them straight;
9, 10,
A big fat hen;
11, 12,
Dig and delve;
13, 14,
Maids a-courting;
15, 16,
Maids in the kitchen;
17, 18,
Maids in waiting;
19, 20,
That's a-plenty.

GAME 1 – One child:
Bounce ball on numbers, pass leg over ball on words.

GAME 2 – Two or more children:
Bounce ball on numbers, toss ball to next child on words.

GAME 3 – Two or more children:
Bounce ball on numbers, bounce-pass to next child on words.

ONE, TWO, THREE O'LEARY

(Tune: Ten Little Indians)

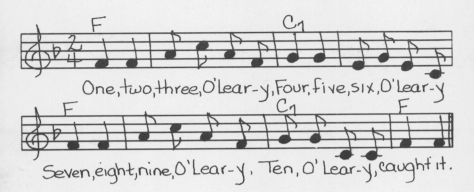

One, two, three, O'Lear-y, Four, five, six, O'Lear-y
Seven, eight, nine, O'Lear-y, Ten, O'Lear-y, caught it.

Formation: One child.

Action: Bounce ball on numbers, pass leg over ball on "O'Leary," catch ball on "caught it."
      (May be chanted instead of sung.)

JACK, JACK

1. Jack, Jack, pump the water;
   Jack, Jack, pump the water;
   Jack, Jack, pump the water;
   Pump the water, Jack.
2. Jack, Jack, jump the water;
3. Jack, Jack, go under the water;

Formation: One child.

Action:
V.1 – Bounce ball in rhythm
V.2 – Pass right leg over ball on "jump"
V.3 – Pass left leg over ball on "under"
      (May be sung to tune of *"Ten Little Indians"*)

ALPHABET BOUNCE

My name is *Alice*,
My husband's name is *Andy*,
We come from *Arkansas*
And we sell *apples*.

Formation: One child.

Action: Bounce ball in rhythm. Pass leg over ball on italic word. Continue through alphabet making up names for each letter.

ONE, TWO, THREE A-TWIRLSY

1. One, two, three a-twirlsy,
   Four, five, six a-twirlsy,
   Seven, eight, nine a-twirlsy,
   Ten, a-twirlsy, catch me!

2. One, two, three a-jumpsy,
3. One, two, three a-crossy,

Formation: One child.

Action: Bounce ball in rhythm
   "twirlsy" – twirl around
   "jumpsy" – jump up
   "crossy" – cross leg over ball

(May be sung to tune of *"Ten Little Indians"*)

ROLL THAT BALL

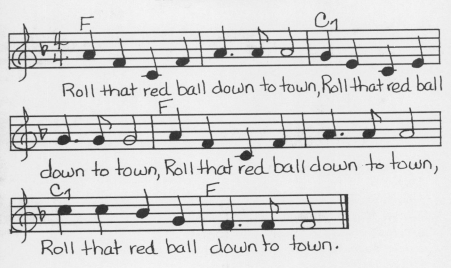

Roll that red ball down to town, Roll that red ball down to town, Roll that red ball down to town, Roll that red ball down to town.

Formation: Children sitting in circle.

Action: Roll ball across circle each time "roll" is sung.

CONCENTRATION

Concentration the letter A,
   Apple begins with the letter A,
Concentration the letter B,
   _____ begins with the letter B,

Continue through the alphabet, bouncing
ball in rhythm.

Suggestion: Game may be played with more than one child,
each taking a new letter.

CATEGORIES

1. Animal, Animal, Animal   (pass)
   Dog, Dog, Dog   (pass)
   Cat, Cat, Cat   (pass)
   Horse, Horse, Horse   (pass)
2. Flower, Flower, Flower   (pass)
   Rose, Rose, Rose   (pass)
   Daisy, Daisy, Daisy   (pass)
   Violet, Violet, Violet,   (pass)

Formation: Circle of players or two
players facing each other.

Action: First child bounces ball in rhythm
as he calls out a category three times
(e.g. animal). On the fourth beat, he passes
the ball to the next child who names something
in that category three times (e.g. dog) as he
bounces the ball. This continues until a
child cannot think of anything else in the
category named, so names a new category
and the game continues.

(Suggested categories – names, months of year,
birds, states, body parts, etc.)

Clap faster AND in rhythm?
.... Who me?

Clapping rhymes

Clapping games are chants or songs with a clapping pattern. They are excellent for developing coordination and a sense of rhythm.

HEAD AND SHOULDERS

1. Head and shoulders, Baby,
   One, two, three.
   Head and shoulders, Baby,
   One, two, three.
   Head and shoulders,
   Head and shoulders,
   Head and shoulders, Baby,
   One, two, three.
2. Knees and ankles, Baby
3. Turn around, Baby
4. Touch the ground, Baby

Formation: Children standing.

Action: Touch body parts when chanted; clap on "one, two, three."

PRETTY LITTLE DUTCH GIRL

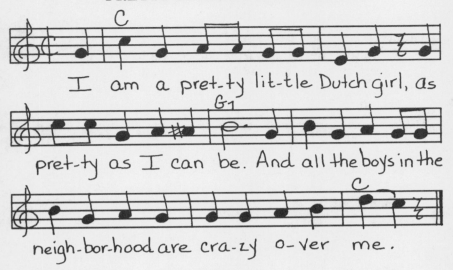

I am a pret-ty lit-tle Dutch girl, as
pret-ty as I can be. And all the boys in the
neigh-bor-hood are cra-zy o-ver me.

2. My boyfriend's name is Mellow,
   He comes from the land of Jello,
With pickles for his toes and a
   cherry for his nose
And that's the way my story goes.

Formation: Partners seated, facing each other.

Action 1:
am – slap knees
pretty – clap own hands
Dutch girl – clap partner's hands
(rest) – clap own hands
Repeat this sequence in rhythm until end of song.

Action 2: (for older children)
am – slap knees
a – clap own hands
pretty – clap right hand with partner
little – clap own hands
Dutch – clap left hand with partner
girl – clap own hands
(rest) – clap partner's hands
as – clap own hands
Repeat this sequence in rhythm until end of song.

WHO STOLE THE COOKIES FROM THE COOKIE JAR?

Group:
> Who stole the cookies from the cookie jar?
> Jimmy stole the cookies from the cookie jar.

Jimmy:
> Who me?

Group:
> Yes, you!

Jimmy:
> Not me!

Group:
> Then who?

Jimmy;
> Linda stole the cookies from the cookie jar.

Linda:
> Who me?

Group:
> Yes, you!

Linda:
> Not me!

Group:
> Then who?

Formation: Group sitting in circle. Decide whose name will be called first.

Action: Chant in rhythm while alternately slapping knees and clapping own hands. Continue chant until all names have been called.

LONG LEGGED SAILOR

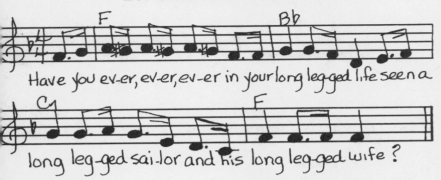

Have you ev-er, ev-er, ev-er in your long leg-ged life seen a long leg-ged sai-lor and his long leg-ged wife?

2. No, I've never, never, never in my long legged life,
   Seen a long legged sailor and his long legged wife.

Formation: Partners seated, facing each other.

Action:
Have you – clap own hands
ever – clap right hand with partner
ever – clap own hands
ever – clap left hand with partner
in your – clap own hands
long – spread own hands apart
legged – clap own hands
life – clap right hand with partner
seen a – clap own hands
long – spread own hands apart
legged – clap own hands
sailor – clap left hand with partner
and his – clap own hands
long – spread own hands apart
legged – clap own hands
wife – clap partner's hands

Repeat for verse 2.

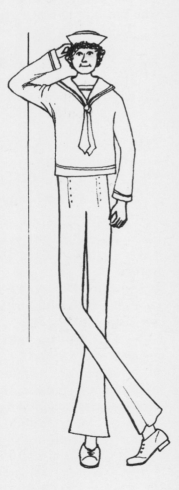

MISS LUCY HAD A BABY

Miss Lucy had a baby,
    She named it Tiny Tim,
She put him in the bathtub
    To see if he could swim.

He drank up all the water,
    He ate up all the soap,
He tried to eat the bathtub,
    But it wouldn't go down his throat.

Miss Lucy called the Doctor,
    Miss Lucy called the Nurse,
Miss Lucy called the lady
    With the alligator purse.

Formation: Partners seated, facing each other.

Action:
Miss – clap own hands
Lu – clap right hand with partner
cy – clap own hands
had – clap left hand with partner
a – clap own hands
ba – clap partner's hands
by – clap own hands
(pause) – clap own hands behind back

Repeat this sequence in rhythm until end of rhyme.

Suggestion: May be sung to tune of
"Pretty Little Dutch Girl."

A SAILOR WENT TO SEA
(Tune: Pretty Little Dutch Girl)

A sai-lor went to sea, sea, sea, To see what he could see, see, see, But all that he could see, see, see, Was the bottom of the deep blue sea, sea, sea.

Formation: Partners seated, facing each other.

Action:
A – clap own hands
sai – clap right hand with partner
lor – clap own hands
went – clap left hand with partner
to – clap own hands
sea, sea, sea – clap partner's hands three times
Repeat this sequence in rhythm until end of song.

Suggestion: On "sea, sea, sea," clap partner's hands, partners clap backs of hands, clap partner's hands.

PEASE PORRIDGE HOT

Pease porridge hot,
Pease porridge cold,
Pease porridge in the pot,
Nine days old.

Some like it hot,
Some like it cold,
Some like it in the pot,
Nine days old.

Daddy likes it hot,
Mommy likes it cold,
I like it in the pot,
Nine days old.

Formation: Partners seated and facing each other.

Action:
pease — slap knees
porridge — clap own hands
hot — clap partner's hands
pease porridge cold — same
pease — slap knees
porridge — clap own hands
in the — clap right hand with partner
pot — clap own hands
nine — clap left hand with partner
days — clap own hands
old — clap partner's hands

PLAYMATE

Say, say, oh play-mate, come out and play with me,
And bring your dol-lies three, Climb up my ap-ple tree,
Cry down my rain barrel, Slide down my cel-lar door,
And we'll be jol-ly friends for-ev-er more.

Formation: Partners seated, facing each other.

Action 1:
Begin on "play –" to do the following motions:
slap knees, clap own hands, clap partner's hands,
clap own hands. Repeat this sequence throughout the song.

Action 2: (for older children)
play – slap knees twice
mate – clap own hands twice
(rest) – clap partner's hands once
come – partners clap backs of hands together once
out – clap partner's hands once
and – clap own hands once
Repeat this sequence in rhythm throughout the song.

HAMBONE

Hambone, Hambone, have you heard?
   Papa's gonna buy me a mockingbird.

If that mockingbird don't sing,
   Papa's gonna buy me a diamond ring.

If that diamond ring don't shine
   Papa's gonna buy me a fishing line.

Hambone, Hambone, where you been?
   Around the world and I'm going again.

Hambone, Hambone, where's your wife?
   In the kitchen cooking rice.

Formation: Seated, clapping independently.

Action:
Lines 1 & 2 – alternate clapping hands and knees
Lines 3 & 4 – alternate clapping hands and thighs
Lines 5 & 6 – alternate clapping hands and chest
Lines 7 & 8 – hands and shoulders
Lines 9 & 10 – hands and head

MISS MARY MAC

1. Miss Mary Mac, Mac, Mac,
   All dressed in black, black, black,
   With silver buttons, buttons, buttons,
   All down her back, back, back.

2. She asked her mother, mother, mother,
   For fifteen cents, cents, cents,
   To see the elephant, elephant, elephant,
   Jump over the fence, fence, fence.

3. He jumped so high, high, high,
   He reached the sky, sky, sky,
   And didn't come back, back, back,
   Till the Fourth of July, ly, ly.

Formation: Partners seated, facing each other.

Action 1: Chant rhyme doing following actions on the last three words of each line.
   Mac – slap knees
   Mac – clap own hands
   Mac – clap partner's hands

Action 2:
Miss – cross arms and slap own shoulders
Mar – uncross arms and slap thighs
y – clap own hands
Mac – clap right hand with partner
(pause) – clap own hands
Mac – clap left hand with partner
(pause) – clap own hands
Mac – clap partner's hands

Continue this sequence for remaining verses.

INDEX

Wee Sing®

by Pamela Conn Beall and Susan Hagen Nipp

Discover all the books and cassettes
in the best-selling WEE SING series!

The above titles are available wherever books are sold or
can be ordered directly from the publisher.

PRICE STERN SLOAN

11150 Olympic Boulevard, Suite 650, Los Angeles, California 90064